FOR ROBERT E. MITCHELL, MY COLLEAGUE

PICTURED BY ROBERT J. LEE

SAMPLED BY NOODLES.

SUPER MIDNIGHT MENU

BY DAVID ELLIOT AT AGE 10.

HOLT, RINEHART AND WINSTON, PUBLISHERS
New York, Toronto, London, Sydney

ISBN: 0-03-047341-1   89012 059 54321

ARCADIA SCHOOL L.M.C.

A pound of salt...

A pOund

of lizards' gizzards...

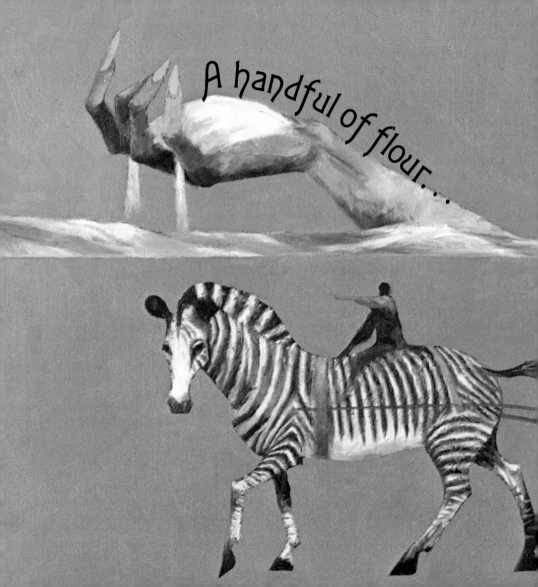
A handful of flour...

Stir for an HOUR...

A pinch

of mustard...

An
inch
of
custard...

A bottle of ink

to make you stink...

A bottle of smoke

to make you choke...

Throw in an old bald tire...

Simmer slowly
on a midnight fire...

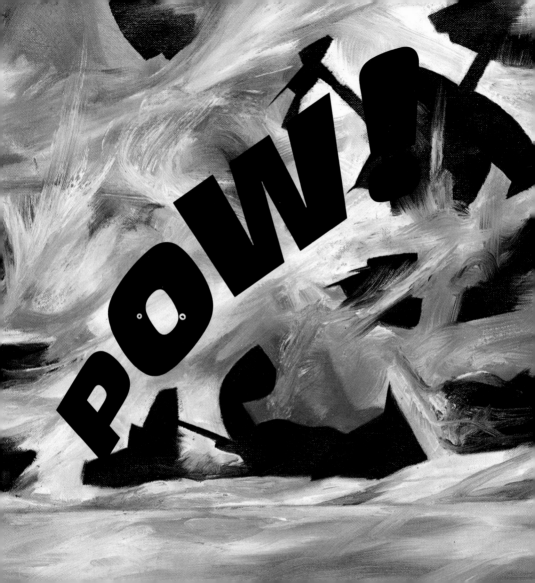